The Princess and the Pea

Jackie Walter and Jane Cope

W
FRANKLIN WATTS
LONDON • SYDNEY

1
A Real Princess

Once upon a time, there was a handsome prince. He lived a life of luxury in a beautiful palace.

The prince had nearly everything that anyone could wish for. He had a splendid horse and the smartest dogs.

He had more gold than he could possibly spend, or even count!

But the prince was lonely. Despite all his riches, he had no one to share them with. He was missing a princess, and a real princess was proving hard to find.

The king and queen wanted their son to be happy, so they decided to help. They made some posters inviting princesses to come and meet the prince. Then the servants put them up all over the kingdom. Surely now the prince would find a real princess to marry.

2
A Princess in a Crowd?

The very next morning, crowds of girls began to arrive at the palace. The prince was known to be kind and brave, and many girls wanted to marry him.

Before long, the guards had to close the palace gates. The prince was baffled that so many girls had come, for his parents had not told him of their poster campaign.

"I just want to meet a princess normally and fall in love," he thought, sadly, as another girl approached him. He met girls from all over the world. And all of them tried hard, but none of them was a real princess.

"This doesn't feel right at all!" thought the prince. "I don't think I'll ever meet my princess." He went to bed feeling lonelier than ever before.

3
The Storm

In the middle of the night, the wind began to howl around the palace, blowing open the king and queen's window.

Soon, lightning flashed and forked through the sky, and thunder rumbled around the grounds. The rain fell in torrents. Still the king and queen slept peacefully. Then there came a thin voice above the noise of the storm. "Please help me!" it cried. "Please let me in! I have nowhere else to go!"

The pleading little voice woke the kindly
king. "Whoever can be out on such a
dreadful night?" he wondered. He pulled on
his boots and went downstairs to investigate.

"Please, somebody, help!" the little voice
called again. The king heard knocking at
the palace gates and he hurried over to
open them.

4
A Visitor

Outside, the king was surprised to find a very cold, wet and bedraggled girl. She was covered in mud and looked absolutely miserable. "Thank you so much for opening the gate," she began. "I'm ever so sorry to disturb you. I'm a princess and my carriage overturned in the storm. I was thrown out and the horses have bolted off with the carriage. Please may I shelter here for the night?"

17

"Of course you may," the king replied and he showed the girl into the palace. He was puzzled. "She certainly does not look like a real princess," he thought to himself, "but she is very polite and she is welcome to rest here until this dreadful storm has passed."

The queen was shocked to see the girl in such a mess. "I've never seen such a sight! Straight into the bath with you, dear!" she ordered. "A princess, indeed," she thought to herself. "We'll soon see about that!"

The queen had an idea to test whether the girl really was a princess. She went to the kitchens and took out a jar of dried peas. "One of these will do," she said, choosing a very hard little pea. "I shall put this pea on her bed and then twenty mattresses shall be put on top of it. If she really is a princess, her skin will be delicate enough to feel the pea through all the mattresses."

By the time the girl had climbed to the very top of all the mattresses, she was very sleepy. "Thank you for your kindness," she called to the king and queen as she crawled into bed, yawning.

Yet despite being so tired, the girl found she
could not sleep. She tossed and turned this
way and that, but no matter what she did,
she just could not get comfortable. She could
feel something in her bed.

5
A Real Princess

The next morning, the queen came into the girl's room asking breezily, "How was your night, dear? Did you sleep well?"

Now, the girl did not want to tell an untruth, but she did not want to appear ungrateful either. So she replied, "Erm, I think I might have hurt my back with the carriage, for whatever I did last night, I just could not get comfortable. It felt as if there was a little lump in my bed."

The king and queen jumped for joy, much to the princess's amusement. "Wonderful!" cheered the king. "Splendid!" crowed the queen. The prince came running in to see what all the noise was about. "We've found a real princess," his parents told him, "and she's really rather lovely! We think you might like each other!"

The king and queen were right and, before too long, the prince and princess had fallen in love. They had a beautiful wedding with the prince's dogs as bridesmaids. The prince never felt lonely again and they lived happily ever after.

About the story

The Princess and the Pea was written by Hans Christian Andersen and was first published in a booklet in 1835. It is based on a story that the author heard as a child.

Hans Christian Andersen was born in Denmark in 1805. He wrote plays, travel books, novels and poems, but he is best remembered for his fairy tales. *The Ugly Duckling* is the most famous of these. *The Princess and the Pea* has been both criticised for showing women as over-sensitive, and praised for making fun of people pretending to be other than who they really are.

Be in the story!

Imagine you are the princess and you have had a terrible night's sleep. How do you feel when you learn that the queen has put a pea in your bed?

Now imagine you are the prince. What do you want to say to your parents when you find out about their test?

Franklin Watts
First published in Great Britain in 2016 by The Watts Publishing Group

Text © Franklin Watts 2016
Illustrations © Jane Cope 2009

A CIP catalogue record for this book is available
from the British Library.

The artwork for this story first appeared in
Hopscotch Fairy Tales: The Princess and the Pea

ISBN 978 1 4451 4653 9 (hbk)
ISBN 978 1 4451 4655 3 (pbk)
ISBN 978 1 4451 4654 6 (library ebook)

Series Editor: Jackie Hamley
Series Advisor: Catherine Glavina
Series Designer: Cathryn Gilbert

Printed in China

Franklin Watts
An imprint of
Hachette Children's Group
Part of The Watts Publishing Group
Carmelite House
50 Victoria Embankment
London EC4Y 0DZ

An Hachette UK Company
www.hachette.co.uk

www.franklinwatts.co.uk